Prelim

In the heart of old Delhi, there were five inseparable friends: Yajur, Balveer, Parth, Kunal, and Sreejesh. They had poured their hearts and souls into a startup idea, "RecAIcle", aiming to revolutionise waste management with AI-powered recycling bins. But after months of pitching their idea to various investors, they had nothing to show for it – no funding, no leads, just a string of rejections. Determined not to let setbacks break their spirits and to clear their mental fog, they decided to embark on an adventurous road trip to Ladakh... a journey that changed their lives!

LEGEND OF THE MYSTICAL CAVE

AYAAN JAIN &
MEGHA JAIN

INDIA • SINGAPORE • MALAYSIA

ISBN
Paperback 979-8-89610-370-7
Hardcase 979-8-89699-363-6

Contents

Chapter 1

The Much-Needed Break

"I couldn't believe my ears! They told me the plan was not creative enough. Can you believe that?" Yajur exclaimed, stuffing his clothes in a duffle bag.

Parth watched the overstuffed bag as Yajur darted from door to dresser, trying to remember everything they would need for the trip.

"What's with your last-minute packing, bro?" Parth asked.

"A few neighbourhood kids had come home to clear their doubts," Yajur explained. "I couldn't say no to them with their exams around the corner."

Yajur had always been a brilliant student, renowned for his exceptional academic prowess in the neighbourhood. His popularity soared when he earned a coveted seat at IIT Delhi. Despite his success, Yajur remained humble and kind-hearted, always willing to lend a helping hand to aspiring students, offering free tutoring and guidance without hesitation.

A whirlwind of activity had transformed Yajur's usually quiet apartment. Just then, Kunal entered the room with a worried expression.

"Can someone tell Balveer to make some room in the car? He's packed it with snacks, drinks, and a giant speaker! It's like we're driving a food truck!" Kunal exclaimed.

"We all know how much he loves food," said Parth. "He needs fuel for his huge body, you see," he added with a grin.

"I guess we owe him at least this much for agreeing to skip his gym," laughed Yajur.

Balveer's love for food was legendary among his friends, but what made it even more impressive was his dedication to fitness. Balveer had been hitting the gym since his teens, and it showed. His towering frame and bulging muscles were a testament to his hard work and discipline. He believed in balancing his love for food with a rigorous workout routine, often saying, "You gotta earn your cheat meals!"

Despite his disciplined lifestyle, Balveer had a soft spot for the homemade delicacies lovingly prepared by his family and friends, especially by Yajur's mother.

"Here, please take these khakhras as well. I made them especially for all of you. They have a good shelf life and are very filling," Yajur's mother said, handing over a round tiffin to Balveer.

"Absolutely, Aunty! You're the best chef ever! I love all your dishes, but khakhras are top-tier," Balveer replied, adding the tiffin to his stash of protein bars. "Don't worry, I'll make sure Yajur and everyone else eat on time."

"Guys, with every passing minute, we're delaying our expected time of arrival by five minutes. We need to get moving to reach our first pit stop by evening," Sreejesh interrupted calmly but firmly.

"Okay, all set! Let's go!" Yajur said, loading the last backpack into his trusty and hardy SUV, his companion – which his father had given him as a graduation present.

"Finally, Ladakh! Here we come!" the friends called out, fuelled by excitement and anticipation, as they rolled out of Delhi's sleeping cityscape.

"Look! The sun is rising over the Aravallis!" Parth said, pointing at the orange hue near the horizon.

"And we are chasing it!" Yajur said, speeding the car onto the national highway.

The journey was filled with laughter, music, and endless stories. They stopped at Chandigarh for breakfast, feasting on delicious parathas and lassi. After another gruelling 8 hours, the gang finally reached the Himalayan foothills. The air grew cooler, and lush forests replaced the city's chaos. They experienced a freedom they hadn't known for a long time as they drove through winding mountain roads and picturesque valleys.

"This is exactly what we needed – a break from those busy schedules, presentations, and madness," Yajur, who was driving, added.

Parth nodded in agreement, stretching his arms. "I feel like hugging these mountains and flying like a bird from the cliff."

Balveer chuckled. "With him around, I don't think we can ever get a break from the madness." Everyone laughed as Balveer increased the volume, letting their favourite song fill the car.

Chapter 2

That Fateful Night!

As they travelled, the boys spent memorable moments at beautiful places like Manali, Rohtang, Keylong, and Jispa. It was their third day, and finally, they were on their way to Leh.

That evening, as the sun dipped below the horizon, casting a golden glow over the rugged landscape, they stumbled upon a charming garden café.

“Can we take a quick break?” Yajur asked.

“I badly need some coffee,” admitted Sreejesh. Soon, they were settled at a corner table of the café, enjoying scrumptious snacks in the mesmerising ambiance as the sky grew darker.

“Good food, good life,” said Balveer, burping unapologetically. Kunal, can you stay away from your DSLR for more than a minute?” Parth challenged.

"I bet he can't," claimed Yajur.

"Jealous people, huh? Photography is an art not everyone is blessed with," Kunal retorted, snapping yet another picture of the sunset.

They lost track of time until Sreejesh jerked from the spark of a cold sensation he felt on his head. "It's going to rain! Quick, let's get back to the car," he shouted, glancing up. Everyone stood up as it began to pour heavily. The group quickly hit the road, determined to reach Leh at the earliest.

"Are we there yet?" Kunal asked.

"He will never grow up!" Sreejesh said mockingly. "He's been asking this on every family trip ever since he started speaking."

Though Kunal and Sreejesh were twin brothers, they had nothing in common. Kunal was very good-looking and was exploring a career in modelling. Sreejesh, on the other hand, was one of the most brilliant students of his batch at IIT Delhi. Their parents were both Physics professors in Kerala.

As they navigated the treacherous terrain, the heavy rainfall and darkness made driving increasingly difficult.

"Careful Yajur! There is a sharp turn to the right!" shouted Parth, tracking Google Maps on his phone.

Suddenly, their car skidded on the wet road and plunged off the edge of a cliff. With sharp branches scratching the windows, the car rumbled down a rocky slope. The world seemed to spin around them, and after a short freefall and a loud thud, the car crashed onto a hard ground.

"Are you all okay?" Yajur asked, looking in the rear-view mirror.

Before anyone could respond to Yajur, Balveer unbuckled his seatbelt, flung open his door to jump out of the car.

"Wait, Balveer, it's dark outside," Parth warned, but too late. As Balveer stepped outside, little did he know he was standing on the edge of a small platform holding the car. He slid down the slope, his scream fading as he fell further downhill.

"Hurry, switch on the flashlights before stepping out of the car," Parth guided. Soon, they all safely got themselves out of the car, balancing carefully within the narrow space on the platform.

"Balveer! Balveer!" Yajur shouted as loud as he could.

"I am here." came a faint voice from below.

Chapter 3

"Is that a Cave?"

"Balveer, are you okay?" Parth called out, trying to peer into the darkness.

"Yeah, but I can't see anything," Balveer's voice echoed back.

"Hang tight, we're coming to get you!" Kunal assured, trying to sound braver than he felt. Despite the initial panic, they stayed calm as Yajur took charge, instructing everyone to stay close and use their flashlights to light the way. Carefully navigating the steep and slippery slope, they communicated constantly to ensure everyone's safety. The sound of drizzling water blended with their voices as they kept descending with determination. Their hearts pounded with exhaustion, fear, and urgency.

Finally, the friends managed to reach Balveer, who was sitting on a rock holding his bruised knee.

"Group hug, guys!" Balveer sighed as Yajur helped him to his feet. There was a sense of relief as they all reunited, dusted off each other, and checked for wounds, taking turns holding the faint flashlights.

"Balveer, you look okay down here. Did you find a secret stash of snacks?" Sreejesh tried to lighten the mood.

"Just enjoyed some quality Me-time while you guys took forever," replied Balveer, laced with sarcasm. "Maybe a few bruises but nothing a good meal can't fix," he added, twisting his arm to check if his elbow was hurt too.

"You gotta earn your cheat meals, right? Well, we'd better find a way out of here first, then we'll go anywhere you say to feast," motivated Parth.

"Deal. But when we go there, I'm driving. Clearly, Yajur's driving skills need some work," mocked Balveer.

"Seriously, guys! I gave you the adventure of your lifetime and you are welcome!" Yajur said, taking a bow. "Now, should we figure out our way out or do you all plan to spend the whole night here blaming me?"

"What's the hotel reception number, Yajur? Can we call them for help?" Sreejesh inquired.

"It's on my phone, but I couldn't find it when we were getting out of the car," explained Yajur, checking his pockets again.

"I have a phone, but it looks like there is no network here," said Parth.

"Mine doesn't have any either," added Kunal, stepping aside to look for any high spots where he might get a signal. Suddenly, he called out, "What's that?" pointing towards a shadowy entrance in the cliffside.

"Is that a cave?" guessed Sreejesh, his curiosity piqued.

They all turned towards the wide, shadowed and serrated entrance, with rough stone walls that were slippery with moisture. A cool, damp breeze drifted out, inviting yet forbidding.

"Should we check it out?" Parth said, stepping closer to Kunal.

"Let's stick together. No more solo adventures, okay?" Yajur warned as the others had already started moving towards the entrance. "Just be careful this time."

"If we find a treasure chest, I'm keeping it," Balveer grinned.

Armed with flashlights and a sense of wonder, the friends ventured inside. The cave was dark and mysterious, with small streams of water trickling down its rocky walls. The entrance merged into a narrow tunnel-like path, forcing them to walk single file. They kept shouting strange voices along the way, pretending to enjoy the echo but secretly hoping to scare away wild dwellers, if there were any.

"Are we there yet?" asked Balveer, mimicking Kunal's accent.

"Stop it! I'm not getting a good vibe. We shouldn't have entered this cave in the first place," cried Kunal.

"Looks like you've been heard. We've hit a dead end, guys," Yajur paused. Just then, the wall on which he leaned for support gave way, revealing an opening.

"Move, let me see," Balveer pushed a few more rocks, pushing his way forward. Soon they found themselves entering a vast, underground chamber filled with strange wall carvings. The air was thick with an otherworldly energy, and they realised they had discovered something extraordinary!

Chapter 4

Divide And Conquer

"Am I dead or what? What is this place?" cried Kunal in disbelief.

"It's incredible!" Sreejesh echoed in excitement.

The friends stood in awe, absorbing the vast chamber with its high ceiling vanishing into darkness. The floor was uneven and dust-covered, the sound of dripping water adding an eerie rhythm. The flickering light of their flashlights cast ghostly shadows, making the strange symbols on the walls dance.

"Do you think this chamber has been hidden here all this time?" Kunal asked.

"It must have been, as it wasn't exactly easy for us to find either," Balveer replied, his chest puffing out with pride.

“I wonder how Prishati would have reacted to these cobwebs and layers of dust,” Parth wondered aloud.

“I bet she would have spent the night cleaning this place down to the last stone,” Yajur laughed.

Prishati, their school friend and another bright student of their batch, had completed her Masters in journalism and was on a hunt for a job at a reputed national daily. Known for her obsessive cleanliness habits, she was popular among the group for her meticulous hygiene practices.

“I have this overwhelming sense of déjà vu. It feels like we’ve been here before! Look at these wall carvings – they’re strange, but I feel they’re trying to convey something important to us,” Sreejesh remarked, his eyes wide with wonder.

“Agreed! Even I find this place familiar, and these carvings are so interesting!” exclaimed Parth, his eyes gleaming with curiosity.

Just then, the sound of rain pouring down heavily outside reached their ears.

“Looks like we’re stuck here for the night. What better way to spend it than trying to figure out what all this means,” Yajur said, looking around at his friends with excitement.

"Yeah! We're going to uncover the secrets of this chamber together," Kunal responded, a newfound zeal in his voice. "I feel like we're in a reality show! Survivor: The Modern Cave Dwellers," he added.

"You guys do whatever you want while I munch on something from this bag you got for me," Balveer said as he sat on a rock against the cave wall.

"We knew you wouldn't die from falling off the cliff. We actually came down to deliver you food," Parth laughed.

"Alright then, let's divide the snacks and the wall sections we'll study based on our interests and expertise," Yajur continued, his voice reverberating through the chamber. Yajur moved closer to the wall on the right, his keen eyes tracing the intricate carvings. "For instance, I pick this wall. These carvings appear to tell something about trade, money, and profit. I am not sure if this is my business acumen or love for money-making, but surprisingly I am able to understand what these drawings are trying to depict," he added with a wry smile.

"I thought cave walls usually had ancient and historical carvings, like something out of the Flintstones, but it appears this isn't just history we're looking at," Parth interrupted, his eyes widening. "These carvings seem to depict events and information beyond our time. The language used, though similar to today's coding languages, is far more advanced. Look at that massive wall over there. It clearly represents an advanced network powered by something like a supercomputer!" His face lit up with excitement.

"I call dibs on that wall!" Sreejesh shouted, leaping forward. "I've been eyeing that wall since we entered. It's packed with images of advanced tech stuff you wouldn't understand in a million years," he teased, yanking Parth's shoulder back as he charged towards the huge wall.

"Speak for yourself. I've already deciphered half of that corner section standing right here. It appears to be a blueprint for portable devices connected to a supercomputer. Network systems and software applications might be your domain, but when it comes to hardware engineering and computer architecture, no one outdoes me," Parth retorted, chasing after Sreejesh.

"How about you both tackle that wall together? Parth can understand the hardware of these devices and Sreejesh can focus on their software," Yajur suggested with a grin, pointing to the section brimming with complex diagrams and advanced machinery. "It's big enough to keep both of you busy for the night."

"I'll decipher that wall as it seems more like the social and organisational structure of those people operating these devices and owning the business," Kunal said, focusing on the left wall with a series of carvings that appeared to outline hierarchies and roles within a society.

Balveer, however, still hung back, taking a bite of his protein bar, and scepticism painted on his face. "I don't get it. Parth and Sreejesh are saying these diagrams of futuristic devices. Yajur's talking about the business model, and Kunal's on about social networks. Since none of these things exist as of now, are we supposed to believe that someone from the future time travelled to this cave, which is hidden below a cliff, carved out their high-tech gadgets, BLAAH...BLAAHH...then vanished – only for us to find it again! Are you even listening to yourselves?" Balveer scoffed, finding a spot to sit in the corner.

"Maybe it was a safe place for them to do so," Yajur mused. "Hidden from enemies or natural disasters."

"Or maybe it was meant to be found by people like us," Parth added with a grin.

"Maybe it's a way to preserve knowledge," Kunal suggested. "Or a time capsule, a method to pass down vital information from future generations to the present."

"Still seems weird to me," Balveer muttered. "If their technology was so advanced and businesses so prosperous, why go to the trouble of time travelling and carving these symbols?" he questioned again.

"Maybe the traveller from the future came back to warn us!" guessed Sreejesh.

"And shared these plans to help us avoid the mistakes that led to their downfall," Parth added, running his fingers over an intricate design.

"Hmmm...still lots of maybes... Wait! I too found something!" Balveer suddenly paused.

"Are you sure? Last time you said those words, it turned out to be your dad's old grocery list," giggled Kunal as they all moved closer to Balveer.

"Doesn't this look like a map of India?" Balveer said, pointing at the wall. "These are the northern mountains, and that's clearly the peninsula," he explained, his confusion giving way to a look of interest.

"Welcome to the league, bro! I know it is way too interesting to resist," Yajur said, smiling at Balveer's growing curiosity.

"Bravo!" Kunal said with an amused slow clap that echoed through the chamber.

"A place towards the eastern region is highlighted with a star. If I'm not wrong, this spot should be somewhere in modern-day Odisha," added Sreejesh, pointing at that side wall.

Chapter 5

Peak Into The Future

The friends spent the night deciphering the images and text on the walls, their minds buzzing with ideas and possibilities. The combination of glittering carvings, the strange echoes of their voices discussing futuristic technology, and the sound of rainwater created a sense of timelessness, as if they had stumbled upon a hidden realm where the past and future intertwined.

Parth and Sreejesh were captivated by the technological diagrams.

“These people are way ahead of our time,” Sreejesh said, breaking the silence.

“Can you explain in simple terms what you geniuses understood from those scribbles?” Balveer asked, sounding unimpressed.

"Okay, tell me, what network does your phone usually operate on?" Sreejesh asked.

"5G network?" Balveer replied with a hint of confusion in his voice.

"Correct," Sreejesh confirmed, turning towards everyone. "Now, the wavelength used in 5G technology, like all electromagnetic waves, has always been around us. So why then have we started using 5G networks only recently?"

"We started using it only after regulatory bodies approved its usage," Parth replied confidently.

"More importantly, deploying a network isn't just about having the right frequencies available. It means creating an entire ecosystem of cutting-edge hardware, software, and protocols. We had to construct sophisticated base stations, design superior antennas, and develop algorithms to tap into the 5G frequencies. Only after building this infrastructure did we begin utilising the 5G network. Simple. Right?" Sreejesh paused, his gaze sweeping over the group to ensure they were all on the same page.

"Similarly, it seems that in the future, they've developed portable devices operating on way more advanced networks, what you could call a 100G network. These gadgets contain advanced processors, superior antennas, and specially designed software to handle such high-frequency networks. They're also connected by a master server above the earth. The speed and precision of data transfer on this network must have been mind-blowing," Sreejesh continued, his excitement clear as day.

"So... you're saying this 100G network already exists today, but we can't use it because our devices aren't advanced enough. Hmm... Interesting!" Balveer mused.

"Exactly. Think of it like solar power. The sun has always been there, but we didn't use it as a source of electricity until we invented solar panels," Sreejesh elaborated, drawing an apt analogy.

"Gotcha!" Balveer replied, a smile of understanding spreading across his face.

"But in the future, these devices are available everywhere. They are even housed at a chain of base stations set up at every nook and corner of the country, where people gather and use them to connect to the master server. You can think of these as public wi-fi and cyber cafés we had back in the 80s. They also organise events and contests, inspiring everyone to constantly upgrade their processors, boosting the development in this area even more," Parth added, providing more details.

"Any information on how we can build these devices?" asked Kunal, joining the discussion.

"Building these devices may not be as difficult as it sounds. While these devices are advanced enough to operate on the 100G network, their hardware is similar to our current mobile phones. What changed the game is the software and microprocessors, which are way more superior and powerful," Parth explained, using the symbols on his side of the largest wall.

"So, can we say this information is promising enough to be our startup idea?" questioned Kunal.

"If we can build these devices or upgrade the existing ones to operate on the 100G network, we could revolutionise the industry. You never know, we might become the founders of this mega empire of the future!" Balveer spoke as he imagined; his voice echoed in the cavernous chamber.

"Hold your horses, Mr. Dreamer!" Parth interrupted.

"It is easier said than done," said Sreejesh.

"Not sure if we alone can do these herculean tasks, but we can always build a team to help us achieve this vision," suggested Kunal.

"Unlike us, the team will not work for you for free," grinned Balveer.

"Other than giving free gym training sessions, what have you ever done for me? Those didn't work either," Kunal retorted, pulling up his T-shirt to show his abs.

"Money shouldn't be an issue. If we can actually make this work, we'll make a lot of money. We can always start small and expand later," Yajur said, his eyes sparkling with excitement.

Chapter 6

The Grand Failure

"What's that on your wall, Kunal? The Pyramids of Giza?" Parth asked, pointing at a triangular diagram.

"Pyramids of Giza? Seriously? This is the organisational structure of the people who built, controlled, and ran this mighty empire of 100G network and these devices," Kunal explained.

"It is similar to a typical corporate or private company of today. It shows an open culture with equality and inclusiveness, and at the same time, people working hard to compete and climb the corporate ladder. The ones at the top lead by example and act in the best interest of the company," he continued.

As the friends went deeper into the cave, the mysterious carvings revealed even more exciting secrets. Parth and Sreejesh gathered around their common torchlight, excitedly pointing out their discoveries and debating the meanings behind each figure. Yajur and Kunal were lost in their own zone too as if they were transported to that era itself. As Yajur, Kunal, Parth, Sreejesh, and Balveer sat together in the dim light, the laughter and chatter that flowed between them mirrored the deepening bond of their friendship. They passed around their snacks, sharing bites and stories, while their minds buzzed with excitement and curiosity about the strange carvings on the cave walls. With each new discovery, the carvings, once cryptic and puzzling, began to unfold like an ancient tale. Their conversations and thoughtful pauses gradually turned the mysterious symbols into a fascinating narrative, each revelation igniting fresh bursts of joy and wonder among the group.

Suddenly, Balveer stood up and called out, as if awakening everyone from their beautiful dreams, "Look at that! There is a huge symbol of danger on this wall!"

"Yes, I saw it too," Yajur acknowledged calmly as he moved towards the last section of the wall and began elaborating. "While the future appears glorious, all of this gradually came to an end. The reasons for this downfall have been listed on this wall with symbols of skulls and bones. Although some lines are faded, what I can make out is that there are three reasons that led to the downfall of this huge industry, turning them into massive losses."

All the friends, including Balveer, followed him, sat near that wall, curious to hear more.

"What could have gone wrong?" Parth had to ask.

"First," Yajur pointed to a symbol of a cyber café, now fading into a coffee cup-like symbol, "they changed their preferences. It seems many people started visiting those cyber cafés not for using the devices to connect to the master server but as a place to hang out and have coffee breaks. Hence, the business of restaurants and cafés replaced the technological advancements, resulting in losses."

"Even I wouldn't prefer coffee over the internet!" said Balveer, puzzled.

"They sought more casual interactions," Yajur explained, "and overlooked the value of learning and constantly upgrading technology."

"Okay, what else?" Sreejesh inquired.

"Second," Yajur continued, showing a corrupted device symbol, "probably a virus corrupted their devices. It was rampant and undetectable, spreading chaos and system outage."

"How did they not see that coming?" Balveer chimed in.

"With a change in preference and a loss of focus, they might have become too complacent," Yajur replied.

"Okay, what more?" Kunal asked impatiently.

"And third," Yajur concluded, pointing to broken network lines amidst smoky clouds, "pollution disrupted their network connections. The air grew thick with pollutants, degrading signals and making connectivity unreliable."

"Has pollution affected the operation of these devices?" wondered Kunal.

"Yes," Yajur nodded, "Never underestimate the environmental impact on any business model."

As his friends sat munching their snacks, their questions brought the lessons of failure from the future to life, resonating with their current lives.

"This could be our chance to turn things around," Yajur said as his voice filled with determination. Parth nodded in agreement.

"If we choose to build something meaningful in this direction, we must ensure we do not repeat these mistakes," Sreejesh declared.

"Agreed!" confirmed Yajur.

"I believe before we decide to become the pioneers of this glorious era, we first need to find our way out of our present dark situation," suggested Balveer.

Chapter 7

Where did DD go?

As the sun began to rise and the rain finally stopped, the friends collected their belongings and made their way out of the cave through a narrow tunnel. They had managed to capture a few images of the carvings before their phones ran out of battery. Soon, they began the tough climb from the depths of the cave back to the road. They carefully climbed up the slippery rocks and narrow ledges, helping each other along the way.

"Want to bet on who'll make it to the top first?" Yajur chuckled.

"I'm in! But we all know who it's gonna be," Balveer joked, flexing his muscles as he pulled himself up another rock.

Soon, they reached the platform and found their broken car. "Guys, any chance we can bring this thing back to life?" Yajur asked, worried about what his dad would say.

Everyone exchanged solemn looks. They decided to salvage essentials and continue their ascent, leaving the car behind as a silent witness to their adventure. Soon, they had climbed their way back onto the road. They quickly sought help from the locals, who offered them warm food and a place to rest.

It took them a few more days to recover and fix their car before they could start their journey back to Delhi. Though they were physically exhausted, their minds were buzzing with a new sense of purpose.

Soon, it was Friday again, and they headed straight for their favourite meeting spot, DD, as they affectionately called it.

Once known as 'Dilli Delights', this charming spot was famed for its signature masala chai and delectable, crumbly kulfi. The shop had seen better days until Yajur's father stepped in during a distress sale, envisioning it as a backup plan for Yajur if high school didn't go well. But Yajur, proving his brilliance, soared through IIT Delhi with flying colours, transforming this once-faded culinary gem into a lively hanging-out destination for his friends.

DD is where Yajur, Parth and Sreejesh had spent hours in group studies, Balveer began his gym training, and Kunal rehearsed his lines for advertisement auditions. It's more than just a place to enjoy; it's their second home where they share their joys, sorrows, dreams, and now their adventure. Each visit is a ritual, a moment of respite from their busy lives. Amidst the chatter and laughter, they find solace and strength in each other's company, making DD a cornerstone of their enduring friendship.

But as they approached the building, they were met with the shocking sight. The entrance was blocked, and a large sign read 'Property seized by bank'.

"What happened here? Why is it locked?" Sreejesh exclaimed, his voice filled with disbelief.

Yajur's face turned pale. "I think I know," he stammered. "I had mortgaged the office space to get some funds for investing in stocks. I thought it would give us the returns we needed but... It didn't work out as expected." Yajur explained with disappointment and guilt in his voice.

Balveer's eyes widened in shock. "You mortgaged DD without telling us?"

"I didn't want to worry you all," Yajur replied with his voice still trembling. "I thought I could handle it, but the investments didn't pay off."

Parth tried to stay calm. "So, what do we do now?"

Sreejesh looked around with his mind racing. "We have got the blueprint of a great business idea from the cave. All we need is a place to work so that we can start putting various components together and build something actionable. We are so close to finally having our own startup. We can't give up now!"

Everyone nodded firmly.

Yajur took a deep breath, guilt and resolve mixing in his expression. "I am so sorry, everyone. I messed up, but I promise I will do everything I can to make it right."

"Chill, bro. We trust you," consoled Kunal.

The friends stood together, their bond stronger than ever despite the setback. With no place to go and their potential office space seized, the friends found themselves at a crossroads.

"How about a quick coffee break, guys?" Parth asked.

"Sure, last time we took a break, we ended up in the cave. Hope this time we don't land somewhere even more adventurous!" Sreejesh said, rolling his eyes.

They went to a nearby café, sipping on hot beverages and brainstorming their next move.

"Hey, remember that map drawn on the cave walls?" Parth spoke, suddenly remembering the map of eastern India they had seen in the cave. "Maybe there's something there that can help us."

Kunal nodded, fetching the image of the map on his phone. "Here it is!" he exclaimed, placing his phone on the table for everyone to see.

"What if we find loads of gold or some kind of treasure! We must visit this place once," Balveer exclaimed in an excited tone.

"I too believe it's worth a shot. We have nothing to lose at least," added Sreejesh.

"I am not sure if we are ready for another adventure. Don't you think we should sort out the DD situation first?" Yajur said, sounding uncertain.

Chapter 8

Another Adventure!

While the friends were debating on whether they should explore the place on the map or not, the café door flung open, and their batchmate, Prishati, walked in, her face beaming with excitement.

"Hey guys! Guess what? I just got a job at Jaago Bharat!" announced Prishati with immense joy and pride in her voice.

"Jaaaago Bhaaarat! Did you get the job of a national rooster?" said Balveer, who doesn't miss a chance to mock Prishati.

"So ironic for someone who herself wakes up at noon," added Kunal, giving a high five to Balveer.

"It is a leading national newspaper publishing agency - for those who do not know. I have been offered the role of a senior journalist, FYI," clarified Prishati glaring at Balveer and Kunal the whole time.

"That's amazing, Prishati! Congratulations!" Parth exclaimed, trying to be as appreciative as possible.

"Thanks, Parth! I guess that's enough about me for today. What's up with you guys?" Prishati asked, recalling their loud discussions when she had entered.

Sreejesh quickly filled her in on the recent adventures and the current predicament.

Prishati listened keenly, her eyes widening with such detail.

"Wow, it's quite a story," Prishati said. "You must check this place out! In fact, I have some vacation time before I start my new job. How about I join you on this trip to eastern India or wherever this place is? I can document the journey and maybe even write an article about it."

"Alright then! Let's go!" Yajur called out, throwing his fist into the air.

The friends matched the coordinates of the real map with the image of the carving. They narrowed down the exact place they needed to visit and agreed on the travel plan. Soon, they were aboard flights to Jharsuguda Airport, a small town in the state of Odisha.

After landing, they travelled a long journey by road to reach the highlighted place on the map of the cave. The trip had been tiring; after hours on a cab, cramped bus, and shared lorry, they were dropped off on the outskirts of a small town. From there, they trekked on foot, navigating through rugged paths and asking the occasional passerby for directions. The closer they got, the fewer people they encountered. To their surprise, it was a village on the edge of a dense forest, far from any modern civilisation.

Residents of the village were dressed in vibrant attire; their bodies adorned with numerous tattoos, and they spoke in an amusing language. As the friends wandered through the village, they asked every villager they encountered about the cave and its carvings. Unfortunately, they were met with nothing but puzzled looks and bizarre responses.

“Have you seen this before?” asked Kunal, showing an image of a carving on his phone to a villager.

“Do you think any of these villagers have ever left this forest, let alone seen that cave?” Prishati asked, her voice dripping with scepticism.

“Excuse me, do you know anything about the cave with these carvings?” Parth asked one villager who responded with a series of hand gestures that looked like a mix between a dance and a mime act.

"Is that a yes or a no?" Sreejesh whispered to Parth, who shrugged in confusion.

Chapter 9

Meeting the Varahmas

The villagers regarded the friends with suspicion and fear, whispering among themselves and pointing at them, making strange expressions.

"Kunal, I feel like the name of your reality show just changed to Survivor: Lost in Translation," Balveer mocked.

Gradually, the villagers became a bit more receptive to listening to what the friends had to ask.

"Maybe they're warming up to us," Prishati suggested optimistically.

"Or maybe they're just curious about our strange clothes," Kunal replied, looking down at his hiking gear.

Despite the villagers' growing curiosity, the language barrier made it difficult for both parties to strike up a meaningful conversation.

"We need a translator to tell them these are cave carvings," Yajur sighed. "Or at least a universal sign for 'cave'."

"How about we draw it?" Prishati suggested, pulling out a notebook and sketching a crude picture of the cave.

The friends showed the drawing to a group of villagers. A young man nodded vigorously and pointed towards the forest.

"I think we've got a lead!" Parth exclaimed.

"Let's hope this doesn't lead us to another cave," Balveer said, rolling his eyes but smiling nonetheless.

"Wait, show the image to that old man," Yajur asked Kunal, pointing to an old villager who was sitting on a tree trunk, perhaps giving some kind of sermon to a group of fellow villagers.

Kunal went and hesitantly stood near the gathering. Unlike other villagers, the old man was dressed in plain yellow, his eyes were wise and kind. Slowly the villagers started getting uncomfortable with Kunal's presence. An awkward silence engulfed the group. The old man looked at Kunal with a smile and gestured for him to come close. Kunal went ahead and offered his phone to the old man, pointing at the images. As he saw one of the images on the screen, the old man stood up and started reciting some strange hymns to the villagers. They began to murmur among themselves and surrounded Kunal. Kunal quickly turned towards his anxiously waiting friends, asking them to follow as the crowd started moving behind the old man.

"I think they are welcoming us," Prishati whispered, her heart pounding with excitement.

The elder led everyone to a large open area where the entire village slowly gathered. The villagers bowed respectfully, and the old man introduced their clan, "We are the 'Varahmas!'"

The friends were glad to finally hear something they could understand. They realised that the villagers saw them as their heroes, possibly due to some prophecy.

Chapter 10

Who is the Guide?

As the friends settled in the open area, the elder who seemed to understand their language spoke in a solemn tone, "Welcome to our village."

"I am Raghav, the elder of the Varahmas. What brings you to our sacred land?" he continued, in a gentle yet commanding voice.

Yajur stepped forward, holding out Kunal's phone with the images from the cave. "We found these carvings in the hidden cave. They seem to depict a successful business model from the future. We came here hoping to learn more."

Raghav studied all the images carefully, a knowing smile forming on his lips. "Ah, I see. What you believe to be a successful business model of the future is actually a failure of the past. These carvings tell the story of a glorious era that gradually faded away."

The friends exchanged puzzled glances.

"Are you sure of what you are saying? How do you know about these carvings?" Sreejesh asked after a pause.

Raghav's expression grew sombre. "Our Guide knows all about the cave and its secrets. He had been teaching us life lessons, guiding us in times of difficulties, and protecting us from the changes that come with time for many years. He also foretold that six modern-looking persons would come someday asking about the cave carvings. I believe he has been waiting for you all."

Prishati's eyes widened in surprise. "So, he knew we would come here?"

"Yes," Raghav replied. "He will explain everything and guide you on your journey."

"Can you tell us a little more about your Guide? Who is he, and how do you know him?" Yajur asked humbly.

"His parents were part of our clan, but they didn't have any children. Then, one day, they found him near the banks of the Mahanadi River. They took him in and raised him as their own. He was brilliant and charming from a young age, often knowing things beyond his age. After his parents were lost in the Odisha super cyclone, he moved to the nearby forest and began spending most of his time meditating. We visit him only on Thursdays, which we call Guruvaar – the Day of Teachers. We compile all our questions for the week, and he answers them all. We keep a book where we note his responses, and it's taught as a reference to every member of our village. Luckily, tomorrow is Thursday. If you'd like, we can take you with us, and you can ask him all your questions."

The friends felt a mix of excitement and appreciation. They had come seeking answers, and it seemed they were about to uncover even more than they anticipated.

"Thank you for welcoming us," Yajur said, bowing respectfully. "We will stay here and meet your Guide tomorrow."

Raghav nodded. "Our village will provide you with shelter and food. Rest well, for tomorrow will be a day of revelations."

Chapter 11

Day of Revelations

As the friends settled into their temporary home, they couldn't help but feel as if the Universe had a plan all along. The journey that had begun with the disappointment of a failed startup and a road trip to Ladakh had led them to the mysterious cave and now to this village, where ancient secrets and future possibilities interconnected.

Until now, they had endless questions swirling in their heads. But the moment they knew they could ask anything and get an answer, their minds went blank! They couldn't figure out what to ask. They huddled together, chatting away, trying to sort and prioritise their questions all night.

The next day, the friends gathered in the village square, their hearts pounding with anticipation.

"While we all shall accompany, only one can speak to the Guide," Raghav informed kindly. "So, who will be the spokesperson among you?"

The friends exchanged confused glances, each one feeling a mix of excitement and anxiety at the prospect of directly interacting with the Guide.

"I'll be the one," Yajur declared confidently, nodding at his friends who silently agreed through shared glances.

"Very well. Follow me," Raghav responded, leading the way towards the entrance of the forest. The group exchanged hopeful looks, ready for what lay ahead.

The friends followed Raghav along with a few more villagers, and after a long walk, they all stopped outside a beautiful hut. Constructed from sturdy bamboo and thatch, it blended seamlessly with its surroundings. A gentle stream nearby sang a soothing melody, while tall ancient trees formed a protective canopy overhead. The entrance of the hut adorned hand-carved symbols of peace and knowledge, resembling those in the cave. The hut's simplicity and harmony with nature reflected the Guide's profound image and serene spirit.

The Guide, a charismatic figure with an aura of wisdom and mystery, emerged gracefully from the hut and approached them. His presence was commanding, and his eyes seemed to hold the secrets of the Universe. Struck silent by his aura, the friends were momentarily tongue-tied.

As the Guide seated himself on a flat tree bark seat and signalled everyone else to be seated, Raghav stepped forward and bowed respectfully. "Greetings, O Guide! Today, we have visitors who are looking for answers from you," he spoke, signalling Yajur to come forward.

Yajur took a deep breath and stepped forward, feeling the weight of responsibility on his shoulders.

The Guide nodded in acknowledgement. "What is it that you seek?" he asked, his voice resonating with a calm authority.

"We discovered these carvings in a hidden cave. They seem to depict codes of advanced technology and a successful business model. Can you tell us more about them?" Yajur asked, showing the images from the cave.

The instant the Guide's eyes fell upon the images, he scanned each friend's face, as if he couldn't quite believe this moment had arrived. When his gaze met Raghav's, he smiled warmly, a smile that seemed to say he was relieved; his long wait to meet these young explorers had finally ended. He then brought his attention back to Yajur and spoke in the utmost divine voice.

"I am glad to meet you, my friend. These carvings that you all have found are treasures of knowledge. However, their interpretation, understanding, and implementation require patience and courage. Please listen to what I say with undivided attention," he said, giving a brief pause.

"Let's start with what you already understand," the Guide began, his voice warm and compassionate. "You're familiar with today's technology – mobile devices, the internet, advances in AI, and so forth. You think these carvings might give you a head start in creating even more advanced devices and networks, leading to a successful business. Have I got that right?" he asked, his eyes twinkling with understanding. Yajur nodded in agreement, feeling impressed with the depth of knowledge the Guide who lives in such a remote forest had about today's world.

"While the carvings do relate to our current technology, they actually represent a glorious era from the past," the Guide continued. "Consider this: the symbols of devices don't represent any futuristic machines but are humans instead - hardware stands for the human body, and software signifies the human mind. The symbol that looks like a battery denotes food, and the protocols symbolise the social norms we live by."

The Guide paused, giving Yajur and his friends a moment to absorb this new perspective.

"How about these numerous base stations located everywhere across the country, where these advanced devices are placed?" Yajur asked, quickly glancing at the other symbols.

"These base stations," the Guide explained with a smile, "are religious places and ancient gurukuls. They were more than just places of worship. They housed immense knowledge and organised intellectual debates, promoting what you might call 'software upgrades' an enhancement of the mind and spirit."

"If devices are humans and the cyber cafés are the holy places, what's the 100G network they are connected by?" Yajur pondered aloud.

"Imagine it as a supremely powerful communication web," Guide replied. "The devices need to be upgraded enough to be able to tap into a network. In the past, it was used more commonly, but gradually it has lost strength. Today it's mostly in the domain of telepathy and those delightful, serendipitous moments when we catch a good vibe." Guide paused. "Anything else you want to know?"

"Yes, what was the trade and business model all about?" Yajur asked.

"It is the most important business of the world - the business of manufacturing thoughts. One must understand the power of the human mind and invest in upgrading the quality of their thoughts. Everything in this world happens twice, first in someone's mind then in reality. Each human has a separate account and is responsible for their thoughts alone."

"That was insightful! Could you also explain what is meant by the downfall of the business and how to avoid it," enquired Yajur anxiously.

"Of course," the Guide began. "Thoughts greatly impact karma – the profitability of the business. If a person speaks well about someone but creates bad thoughts for them, they create bad karma, leading to business losses. Similarly, good deeds done with bad intentions also result in losses. The downfall of a business is often explained as a lack of mechanisms to produce positive thoughts. The lesser the frequency of good thoughts, the poorer the business is."

"To avoid going into that situation of failure to create good thoughts, the primary requirement is a healthy and strong mind. Just as maintaining a strong body requires a good diet, regular exercise, and immunity to illness, the same applies to the mind.

Feeding it with moral values and positivity every day is crucial. Can't overindulge one day and starve the next," the Guide continued with a smile.

"Building immunity from viruses like ego, negative attitude, comparisons, jealousy, greed, and attachment helps a long way. Avoiding the pollution of repetitive and useless thoughts – often from overthinking the past or future - is very important. Constant exposure to junk and toxic information is a significant threat to the prosperity of the good-thought-making business. Acknowledging any issues and seeking necessary therapy ensures a healthy mind," the Guide elaborated.

"Sure! All of it makes sense. Lastly, could you help us decode what this master server is that people gathered to connect with at these cafés?" Yajur asked.

The Guide, raising both hands upward and giving a serene smile, responded, "I believe you already have the answer, my friend. Visiting holy places to connect with this master server is a good idea, but at the same time not falling into the trap of superficiality is important." After a thoughtful pause, he added, "I suggest you revisit the carvings, now enlightened by our conversation. Then, return with any new questions that ignite your curiosity."

As the friends took a moment to process everything, the massive challenge ahead became clear. They needed to dig deeper into understanding the human mind and its capabilities. Raghav glanced at them and gave a nod, signalling that their time with the Guide was up. Feeling a bit overwhelmed by their new perspective, they stood up and said goodbye to the Guide, who slowly walked back to his hut.

Chapter 12

Bidding Goodbye

As Yajur and his friends walked back from the forest, each was lost in thought after their profound meeting with the Guide. When they reached the village square, Prishati broke the silence.

"What an experience! I'm so glad I came along; I would have missed out big time."

"You are the queen of FOMO, after all," Balveer chuckled.

"I can't get that smiling face of the Guide out of my mind. But, wow, that smile was really something," Prishati remarked.

"Though we tried our best to interpret the carvings, we were way off from their actual meanings. Those 'devices' were humans, the 'cyber cafés' were spiritual places, the 'business model' was about constructing meaningful thoughts, and the 'grand failure' was the downfall of an entire era due to a gradual decline in the ability to create positivity," Yajur summarised.

"Looks like his brain just got a software upgrade," Balveer whispered softly to Kunal.

"I heard that, Balveer," Yajur paused. "Even if it may not be a startup idea anymore, the knowledge we received is very precious. We should at least fully understand the message," he suggested.

His encouraging words resonated with everyone, and they all agreed. Soon, they gathered in their lantern-lit room.

"Last time we studied the structure of the human brain was in the school's biology class. Remember how Nilima ma'am used to scold you for your pathetic diagrams?" Prishati said, pointing at Balveer.

"It must be your fault. Most of the diagrams in my notebook were made by you," Balveer laughed.

"I bet none of us has studied or thought about the brain and its powers in this manner before," Yajur pointed out.

"No wonder! What we thought of creating in the future already existed in the past in the form of human brains – great processing speed, the ability to learn, comprehend, and make decisions," Parth added.

"So true! The comparison with the mobile phone was epic. I was thinking, just like our phones get hung up if we don't delete old and useless data, so does our mind. Isn't it?" Prishati added.

Kunal joined in, "In my industry, people are so conscious about their appearances and quite ignorant of what's inside. It's like caring only about the beauty of a mobile cover and wallpaper while ignoring the software and operating system. It's so hilarious!"

"Can't agree more! Today there are salons, gyms, fashion outlets, so much for the hardware and body of 'devices' but unfortunately similar importance is not given to the software and the operating system that runs the 'devices'," Parth said, supporting the idea.

"I guess that's because 'what's seen is sold.' We see the body, but we don't see the mind. As the Guide said, whatever is created is first conceptualised in someone's mind, then in reality. Be it the fastest quantum computing chip, the deadliest weapons, beautiful artwork, the tallest buildings and even the artificial intelligence systems.. And yet, the mind is often neglected," Sreejesh added.

"I understand the whole 'body as hardware, mind as software' analogy, but 'food as the battery'? Seriously?" Balveer questioned.

"I think the Guide meant we should keep ourselves 'charged' at optimal levels, just like our devices. We should eat between 40% and 80% of our capacity for the best performance," Sreejesh explained, seeing things in a new light.

"Okay, that makes sense. But what about the 100G network?" Prishati wondered.

"It seems like an invisible web connecting one human brain to another," Yajur added.

"Is that even possible?" Balveer asked, sceptical.

"Remember before we had mobile networks and phones, people would have reacted the same way if someone told them they could communicate wirelessly across the globe," Sreejesh pointed out. "Sharks don't know camels exist."

"Absolutely. And let's be real, we've all tapped into this network at some point. You know, like when you get a call from someone just as you're thinking about them or read someone's mind even when they didn't say a word. What else could that be?" Parth said, with a smile.

"I read somewhere about scientists studying the brain waves and their types, but I never imagined these waves as an entire wi-fi network," Kunal wondered aloud.

"Remember the Guide mentioned, we need to be upgraded enough to access it," Yajur explained.

"Can we still upgrade our minds?" Kunal asked.

"Good question. I'll note it down to ask the Guide next time," Parth said, pulling out his tablet.

"Next time? Are you planning to stay here until next Thursday?" Prishati asked, surprised.

"Not just next, a few more if required," Parth said confidently. "There's still so much to learn."

Just then Kunal received a call. "It's from the advertising agency. They want me for a shoot," he said, excitement and hesitation in his voice.

"And I need to start my new job as well," Prishati added, looking torn between her responsibilities and adventure.

The friends knew they had to make difficult choices. With heavy hearts, they decided that all except Parth would return to Delhi the next morning. They chatted till late that night, laughing and discussing every possible detail. They hugged each other tightly before retiring for the day.

Next morning, as Parth watched his friends leave, he felt calm and resolved.

"Are you sure you would be safe here?" Balveer asked.

"I hope the next time we meet you are not miming like them," Sreejesh remarked.

"Take care of yourself, Parth. Keep us posted on what you get to know from the Guide," Prishati said.

"Here, take my spare mobile; you never know, you might need it," Yajur offered.

"Thanks, Yajur," Parth said, keeping the phone.

"Had I not been receiving calls from the bank officials, I would have stayed back," Yajur said in a sombre tone.

"Don't worry about me, guys. I'll be fine. You all have a safe journey. Text me when you reach, and do let me know when we have our DD back," Parth said waving goodbye to everyone.

He knew his path to understanding the human mind and uncovering the secrets of the past would be long and tough, but he was determined to see it through. He quickly grabbed his tablet and started reviewing the questions he had noted for the Guide.

Chapter 13

Time to Change, Parth

The village of Varahmas was a haven of tranquillity and ancient wisdom. Parth quickly became immersed in the villagers' daily life, learning their routines and traditions. They welcomed him warmly, treating him as one of their own.

Lacking a continuous electricity supply in the village, Parth travelled to the nearby town to charge both Yajur's and his phones whenever he could. Despite this arrangement, he still spent much time without a phone. This downtime turned into a blessing, allowing him to explore the lush forest, build connections with the villagers, participate in communal tasks, and learn their language. He realised this journey was transforming him in ways he had never imagined.

He learned to appreciate the simple joys of life, the importance of community, and the power of ancient wisdom. One of the most fascinating parts of his stay was learning from Raghav, the village elder. Raghav shared not only the Varahmas' history and ancient knowledge but also practical life lessons.

"You know, Parth, the night sky is a bit of an illusion. The light from the stars you're seeing now was actually emitted millions of years ago. What you're seeing is the light that has just reached your eyes, but those stars may or may not still exist where they appear," Raghav told Parth as they stargazed. "I never thought of it that way!" Parth said with a twinkle in his eyes.

In the evenings, Parth would sit by the fire with the villagers, captivated by their songs and stories of heroic deeds and the boundless wisdom of their leader, Raghav. They shared how Raghav single-handedly protected them during the super cyclone, taught wise irrigation techniques to prevent floods, and fostered bonds with animals.

Every Thursday, Parth met with the Guide who revealed more about the carvings and their true messages. These conversations unveiled that the cyber cafés in the cave carvings were actually religious sites where people gathered to share knowledge. These places served as libraries and community centres for debates and discussions, inspiring intellectual excellence and divine connection.

"Though these sacred sites exist today, they've become mere shadows, places where rituals are performed without understanding their deeper significance," the Guide sighed, looking at Parth. "It's like the cyber cafés that were once hubs of powerful networks, now turned into coffee houses devoid of internet connectivity," he added, drawing an analogy that resonated with the young listener.

Parth also learned more about the reasons for that era's fall. He questioned and sought detailed explanations on elements like the virus and pollution, symbolising negative thinking and moral confusion.

While Parth was immersed in his study, he received weekly updates from his friends. Kunal's advertising shoot was a success, Prishati was thriving in her new job, Yajur had managed to recover funds and rescue their DD. Sreejesh completed his application developer course, and Balveer got a contract for the supply of gym equipment to a chain of fitness centres. Despite the distance, their bond remained strong, and they continued to encourage and inspire each other.

As the weeks passed, Parth's understanding of the human mind and its potential deepened. He began to see how his knowledge could be applied to develop yet another startup idea! He felt as if all the pieces of his experiences had come together into a beautiful and clear picture. He knew that the journey ahead would be challenging, but his stay in the village had made him ready to face anything with determination and resilience.

While he had always been excited for his weekly catchups with his friends, this one was different. He reached his usual place in the town early, charged his cell phone, and made himself comfortable in a corner. As soon as his watch showed their usual meeting time, he quickly switched on his phone and connected to their conference call.

"Guys, I have something exciting to share with you all!" Parth spoke as soon as everyone joined the call.

Chapter 14

Startup, Again!

The friends were thrilled to hear Parth's happy voice, especially since they hadn't met him in a while. His excitement sparked curiosity in all of them. What could Parth be about to say?

"Don't tell me you're getting married to a girl from that Varahmas village," teased Prishati.

"Those guys might still be practising dowry. Ask them for at least two buffaloes," Balveer laughed.

"Can you all be serious, for once?" Parth said, sounding a bit disappointed and embarrassed.

"What is it, Parth? We're all ears. Tell us what's got you so excited!" Yajur intervened, trying to encourage him.

"I finally have a startup idea that is complete and will definitely work for us!" Parth declared. "We now are aware that it is the mind that needs to be upgraded. Let's enable everyone to do it by providing them with both digital and offline platforms. We'll digitise the knowledge we got from the Guide, build an app for users to access, practice, discuss, and compete on their journey to upgrade the minds. We will also build a chain of wellness centres for the mind," he continued.

"Just like we have gyms and fitness centres, Zumba, Yoga, Pilates, Planks and so on for physical fitness," Parth continued, "we need to create countless options for building mental, emotional, and spiritual fitness."

"It can also be like salons for grooming the mind!" Prishati imagined.

"We must have multiple diet plans such as high fibre and low carb, keto diet, intermittent fasting, microgreens for nourishing the mind too!" wondered Balveer.

"I get it. It's like trying to upgrade a computer by only beautifying the hardware without updating the operating system – we won't see real progress until we move from MS-DOS to Windows. Parth's business idea is about creating brain workout routines, mental diet plans, and platforms to enhance mental well-being and productivity. But do any of these concepts actually exist?" Yajur questioned.

"While there are already some excellent resources out there, we'll bring everything under one umbrella and make it accessible to the masses," Parth added. After a pause, Parth exclaimed with a gleam in his eye, "We can finally be the pioneers of a new era!"

"Sounds really intriguing," Yajur agreed. "We can think this through and make something out of it."

"We could open a chain of MWCs—Mind Workout Centres—within the gyms and fitness centres. It would be perfect for those who prefer offline mind workout sessions," Balveer suggested.

"I can arrange for a permanent column on mental health in our daily. It could help promote our initiative to the masses," Prishati added.

"Once we've built the app, we can digitise all the knowledge from the Guide and create advanced AI systems to mimic him to help solve people's problems," Sreejesh thought aloud.

"I can bring in celebrity clients and influencers to market the app and training centre," Kunal pitched in.

"Awesome team! Sounds like a plan!" Parth exclaimed.

"Let's each do some groundwork in our areas and see how far we can push this idea before our next meeting," Yajur said, inspiring everyone to make progress.

As we wrap up, let's remember to prioritise the well-being of our users, the community, and the environment. I've learned a valuable lesson from these villagers: when our intention is to help others get better, we start enjoying the task and, as a result, perform better at it. It is not what we do but how we do that defines our success. Let's keep that in mind as we move forward," Parth concluded.

"Looks like we have a new Guide in town!" Kunal laughed.

"He has already started speaking with us weekly," Balveer continued the mockery.

"Some people never change! Hope to see some progress when we catch up next!" Parth said as they disconnected the call.

Chapter 15

A Valuable Lesson for Sreejesh

One afternoon, while Parth was sitting by a bubbling brook, he switched on his phone to check an image of the cave. He saw a message from Sreejesh, "Call when free, not urgent." Parth decided to respond immediately.

"Parth, hope I am not bothering you," Sreejesh's voice came with a little hesitation. "I was thinking about the development of the mobile application you mentioned the other day, and I'm stuck. I need some advice on how to upgrade one's mind."

"Of course, Sreejesh. It's the first question on my list for the next meeting with the Guide. I knew you would want it but didn't know you were already on it!" Parth replied.

"Yup, I am ahead of you, as always!" Sreejesh boasted. "Is it possible that you keep me on call when you talk..." Sreejesh spoke, but the call dropped. "No network!" both spoke to themselves but felt as if they heard each other. Brain network, is it? Both smiled.

Next day, as Parth reached where the wise figure was meditating, Parth explained the situation, and the Guide opened his eyes, a twinkle of amusement in them.

"Ah, developing a mobile application, you say? To upgrade the mind? Interesting! Let me tell you the five essential principles that were followed in ancient times," the Guide began, his voice calm and resonant.

"First, maintenance of inner temperature. Just as any supercomputer needs an optimum temperature to function, so does the mind. Encourage users to find and maintain their inner equilibrium."

"Second, do something new and different. Agility of mind comes from embracing change and novelty. Incorporate features that challenge users to step out of their comfort zone, learn something new or try different possibilities."

Parth nodded, jotting down notes. "Got it. What's next?"

"Third, do something constructive for the environment and community. True well-being comes from contributing to the greater good. Integrate activities that promote environmental consciousness and community service."

"I totally agree with this. What's the fourth principle?" Parth said with visible curiosity.

"Accept, forgive, and express gratitude. These are the pillars of resilience. Include features that encourage users to reflect on their experiences, forgive themselves and others, and practice gratitude."

Parth's voice softened. "That's beautiful. And the fifth?"

"Stay true to oneself and focused on one's own karma. Authenticity and self-awareness are key to a fulfilled life. What goes around definitely comes around. Design the app to help users focus on their own actions and stay aligned with their values."

Parth finished taking notes and thanked the Guide. "This is incredible. It sounds like these principles will help build the layout of the app. Thank you!"

The Guide nodded. "One more thing: following all the attributes is not an easy task and requires a lot of inner strength. Make sure to provide a good diet for the mind to be consumed daily. This will help users build a mind strong enough to perform the above tasks. However, guarding the mind against toxic and irrelevant information is equally important. Seeds of the best quality do not grow in soil full of weeds," the Guide said with a smile, then closed his eyes again.

Back in Delhi, Sreejesh integrated the Guide's principles that Parth shared with him into the mobile application he was working on. He collated simple games to help users maintain their inner temperature, created prompts that motivated users to embrace new challenges, added suggestions to visit events and local initiatives to make a positive contribution to society, suggested videos to practice gratitude, and sent reminders to stay true to themselves. He felt the app gained some shape and would resonate with the users.

"I am going to add push notifications with motivational quotes and questions like '*If you are worried about the future, it's because you are wasting your today*' or '*Were you kind to a stranger today?*'. There would also be thought-provoking fun facts, such as '*You created 60,000 thoughts yesterday, but most of them were the same as the day before yesterday. Try creating some new ones today!*' How does it sound?" Sreejesh asked as he updated Parth on the progress.

"Good going, champ!" Parth appreciated.

"Did Yajur tell you he has finalised the plan to convert DD into our first offline mind workout centre?" Sreejesh asked. "He has also started pitching to prospective investors for funds to renovate DD into the centre."

"I didn't know that! Amazing news! With all his business contacts, I'm sure he will sort it out soon." Parth exclaimed.

"I agree. Alright, Parth, catch you later. Take care." Sreejesh said.

That midnight, Parth suddenly woke up from his sleep as he heard something ringing. It was his phone's ringtone. He missed the call as he struggled to reach out to his phone in complete darkness. He saw the screen with one eye as it was too bright. The phone beeped – low battery, only 5% was left. Who would have called me at 1 am and why?

He opened the call history. It was Yajur!

Chapter 16

Yajur Gets Help

"Parth, I need your help," Yajur said, his voice tinged with disappointment. "Tomorrow, I have an investor meeting for our wellness centre. An insider informed me today that if our business model doesn't include a food outlet, the funding won't be approved. I really don't have time to integrate a strong food brand into the plan now. Besides, I believe it would turn our centre into just another food joint or café. Our focus should be solely on mind enhancement."

Parth sensed something was off. "Where are you right now, Yajur?"

"At DD," came the reply.

"Why DD at this hour?" Parth asked.

"I don't feel like going home. I'm sleeping here tonight," Yajur sighed.

"Why? What happened?" Parth sounded concerned.

"I had a fight with my mom this morning. You know how she's always so concerned about my diet and meals. Today, she stood at the door with a glass of milk and wouldn't let me leave until I drank it," Yajur explained.

"Moms and their food concerns, huh? Classic," Parth chuckled, trying to lighten the mood.

"I was already late for the meeting, and somehow, my anger got the best of me. I threw the glass on the floor. It's really bothering me now," Yajur admitted. "And then these crazy demands from investors just added to the stress."

Parth noticed his phone battery was now at 1%. "Yajur, I just forwarded you something I shared with Sreejesh for his app. These are notes from one of my meetings with the Guide. Read them and see if it helps. Let's connect tomorrow during our weekly catch-up and discuss in detail. My phone could shut off any moment..."

Parth stopped as he heard the shutting-down ringtone.

That night, Yajur sat alone at DD, pondering over Parth's message. The five principles resonated deeply within him, shifting his perspective. "Maintain inner temperature...do something new and different... contribute to the community...accept, forgive, and express gratitude...focus on one's own karma," Yajur muttered, analysing each principle in his mind.

As the night wore on, Yajur found peace with his mother's concerns, feeling grateful for her unwavering love and care. He embraced inner tranquillity and accepted the situation. With this newfound clarity, an innovative idea began to take shape in his mind.

The next morning, Yajur returned home and hugged his mother. "Mom, I am so sorry about yesterday!" he said, his voice full of regret.

"It's alright, my son," she replied in a teary voice. "Where were you last night? Did you have dinner? You look so tired, son."

"I am fine, Mom. I was at DD, trying to figure out how to make our business plan appealing to the investors. I found out that they won't back us unless we include a food outlet in our centre. And I don't want it to just become a place to hang out and eat. So, I've come up with a plan," Yajur explained.

"You make the world's best theplas and khakhras, and your friends are good at cooking too. You have told me many times that you need some meaningful engagement every day. Hence, rather than having any fast-food chain, can you and your friends help us?" he asked, hesitantly.

"Anything for you, my son. Tell me, what is it that you want?" she comforted.

"I understand that being homemakers, your presence at home is essential. But I believe sparing 2-3 hours a day should be manageable, right?" Yajur asked.

"Absolutely!" she agreed.

"Perfect! Just gather a group of your friends and have two moms take turns preparing one meal a day for the customers. This way, we'll have fresh, healthy food infused with motherly love, spreading warmth throughout the community, and no single mom will be overburdened. We'll hire staff to handle serving and billing, ensuring everything runs smoothly and seamlessly."

His mother's eyes lit up with excitement. "That's a wonderful idea, Yajur! My friends and I would love to help. So, you'll need six moms in total, including me – two per meal. That should be no problem at all. And don't worry about the kitchen setup; we've got it covered." Yajur's mom proclaimed confidently.

"Thanks, Mom! Love you!" said Yajur as he hugged his mother as tightly as he could.

With renewed enthusiasm, Yajur presented the revamped business model to the investors. He highlighted that the wellness centre would feature a kitchen offering nutritious, freshly cooked meals infused with warmth and compassion, promoting both physical and mental well-being. The investors were impressed by the holistic approach and approved the funding.

Later, on the weekly team call, Yajur shared the good news. "The Wellness Centre is now official! The investors loved the idea, and we got the funding! We are starting with renovation of DD next week. Thanks, Parth, for sharing those principles. They really made a difference."

Parth laughed. "I'm glad to hear that, Yajur. It's amazing what a little wisdom and a lot of love can achieve," he knew that the Guide's teachings would always be a guiding light, not just for him, but for others too...

"Trust me, guys, I am super happy for our first wellness centre. But I have a major problem," Balveer said, his voice laced with disappointment.

Chapter 17

Balveer Gets Stuck

In his next meeting with the Guide, Parth began with the challenges Balveer was facing, hoping for some wisdom and guidance. "In our last working group meeting, Balveer provided an update regarding his discussions with gym owners to whom he is currently supplying equipment. He tried his best to convince them to sublet half of their space for MWC, but the gym owners didn't see much value in the idea and were only ready to provide less than 20% of the total space," Parth said, sounding a bit troubled.

"Considering how enthusiastic Balveer was about this idea, the gym owners' nonchalance hit him hard, and he is extremely disappointed. He doesn't think the small space would be enough to achieve the outcome we set out for," Parth added with a warm sigh to seek guidance.

"Disappointments are stepping stones for success to come. Furthermore, however small a place may be or however unimportant a job may be, all one needs to do is to give their best and success would eventually follow. Good things often take time!" Guide uttered with his ever so calming voice.

When Parth wanted some more clarification, the Guide added, "Big things are mostly created with small steps, and perseverance is key. It is also important to be agile and be able to adapt."

After a few more questions, Parth seemed convinced and confident to discuss this further with the group.

In the next working group meeting, Parth started the discussion, "Balveer, regarding your predicament, based on my interaction with the Guide, we should explore the idea of small spaces with gym owners and the possibility that this helps us start in the right direction with the ability to scale once everyone tastes success."

Balveer was still struck with disappointment. "I already worked out the mathematics, and it does not give us the right commercial outcome," he replied.

"No door is closed until we decide to turn our back on it," Parth said to Balveer, pointing out that this was the Guide's final message.

"I agree. Even the prayer rooms at the airports and hotels are small but have gone on to become a great success eventually," added Kunal.

"Try to work on the commercials again with some toned-down expectations," Yajur suggested. "Let me connect separately with you after the call."

After hearing all the messages from Parth and getting support from others, Balveer looked visibly inspired. He set his ego aside and embraced the small beginning with grace and complete dedication. He realised - what matters is not what you do but being the best at doing it.

"Guys, why is Prishati not on the call today?" Parth inquired.

"She said she was occupied with something, so will attend the next one." Kunal replied.

Chapter 18

Kunal Faces A 'Reel' Challenge

It was 7 am on Wednesday morning, and Parth's phone rang even before the 8 am alarm he had set the phone for every Thursday. He hurriedly picked up the phone, accidentally knocking his water bottle to the ground.

"Hey Kunal, why are you calling me this early?" Parth enquired, still rubbing his eyes to adjust to the light in the room.

"Good morning, Parth. I know it is a bit early, but I hope you can talk," replied Kunal.

Sensing worry in Kunal's voice, Parth assured him to continue to elaborate.

"I am travelling today for a shoot, so I wanted to share something that has been bothering me recently. Please consider checking on it with the Guide today, though I am unsure whether he would be aware of today's social media menace," Kunal continued.

"Go ahead, Kunal! I will definitely run it by the Guide. I am sure he will have some helpful words," Parth assured.

"I am conflicted in my mind about the road to success. In my domain of modelling and influencers, day by day, there is an increased sense of competition which is giving rise to malpractices. My fellow colleagues view me as their competition and to succeed they are resorting to unfair practices like buying paid followers on social media, erroneously editing videos via AI, and making wrong claims about promoting certain unhealthy products. And still, the viewers are cheering for them, and they are being showered with money and fame. This is affecting me, as my numbers are dwindling, and my deals and connections are being offered to them. There is so much ignorance in the viewers that plain visible truth is missing their attention." Taking a deep breath, Kunal concluded, "Maybe they are right. In today's world the road to success is a bit twisted and does involve using unfair means every now and then. In the end, success is what matters, right?"

Parth patiently listened to Kunal and calmed him down without providing any view on his questions but assuring him that there's definitely merit in his questions and his worries are not misplaced. He promised to get back to Kunal with some guidance from the Guide.

In the next working group meeting, Prishati was again not present, which was concerning for the team, but they all agreed to check in on her later in the day.

The first item on the agenda was to address Kunal's concerns. Parth started, "I had a very meaningful conversation with the Guide earlier in the week. I provided a detailed account of Kunal's concerns and, to my surprise, the Guide was glad to hear about it. He mentioned that he expected these concerns to be raised much earlier."

Parth continued to share insights from his conversation, "He clearly articulated that the true test of any human being is how they respond to, and not react to, adverse circumstances. When faced with fear or competition, do you work hard to improve or do you take shortcuts to success? A student who cheats in an exam to become a civil engineer will ultimately be able to build a bridge that would last only months, facing graver consequences than failing an exam."

Kunal wasn't convinced. "I said he wouldn't understand today's competition, and perhaps I was right."

"Hear me out, Kunal. Referring directly to today's world of social media, he clearly called out that the only approval or likes one needs is from themselves and their loved ones. The number of likes or followers may decide the amount of money one makes but cannot bring the inner peace and happiness one gathers from self-approval. To choose shortcuts to money by promoting unhealthy products is a steep downhill slope to disaster, and the outcomes are often not immediately visible but are grave. A big part of success lies in good health, inner peace, and overall wellness. Never underestimate the power of good karma," Parth continued.

Parth further convinced Kunal to continue his journey with honesty and tenacity and to continue to support healthy brands on his social media. He suggested some newer marketing techniques of combining funny content with his brand promo videos which may expand his reach to a wider audience. He also advised Kunal to add multilingual support to his content so that his content reaches even the parts of rural India which are as much connected with the internet as the urban areas.

"Speak what you believe, and you shall never regret; do good to others and you shall never fail; be the best version of yourself and you will never be forgotten," Parth concluded.

"It does make me feel better and confident. Now that I am not focusing on others, I am getting many creative ideas for my own work," admitted Kunal.

For the next item on the agenda, Balveer provided an update.

"Guys! The idea of small spaces in gyms for mindfulness centres has become a hit!" Balveer exclaimed, as if he were eagerly waiting for his turn to speak.

"Are they killing mosquitoes? 'Hit'...brand of pest control...no...? Sorry, continue..." Sreejesh tried to crack a joke.

"The small spaces are not that small anymore. Let me explain, see, in the first half of the day we do use it for its intended purpose, but then during noon time, we have added some more space for the moms' kitchen idea. So instead of bulking on artificial and body-harming steroids, the customers are flocking to mouth-watering freshly prepared diets enriched with protein and natural strength supplements. We have seen our footfall quadruple in just a week, revenues closing in on more than 20% of the entire gym," Balveer said, visibly excited with the progress.

"Hope you yourself are not the major consumer of moms' kitchen," mocked Parth.

"I knew this was your plan all along, to have easy access to my mom's khakhras," commented Yajur.

Everyone congratulated Balveer on his success and wished him luck to continue with caution and not get complacent. Next, it was Sreejesh who wanted to share his story.

"Our app has hit 20K downloads with more than 80% active users. We have offered a 1-month complementary membership to our offline centre for referrals. This will boost both new online subscriptions and footfall at our MWC," Sreejesh updated.

"Good going, guys!" Parth appreciated.

While the call was concluded on a happy note, everyone was reminded to check in with Prishati.

Chapter 19

Prishati Is Lost

After their last call, everyone had been trying to reach Prishati, but to no avail. She wasn't picking up their calls, and texts went unanswered. They came to know she continued going to work, yet she skipped their weekly calls. When Kunal and Balveer tried visiting her house, she didn't even answer the doorbell and turned up the television to avoid hearing their voices.

That's when Parth called one of Prishati's work friends to inquire about her. Her friend was glad someone was worried about her and explained that Prishati had been engulfed by the web of pessimism and negativity that were rampant in the news and social media.

Her friend revealed that Prishati had been reading extensively about wars, pandemics, religious divides, and other distressing topics, which were poisoning her mind. Consequently, she had become an introvert and confined herself, her faith in the goodness of the world and the prosperity of the mind significantly shaken. She also mentioned that Prishati might be on the verge of suffering from depression and might need medical assistance soon.

After talking to Prishati's friend, Parth realised there was no time to waste. He immediately went to Raghav and insisted on meeting with the Guide. Raghav reminded Parth that it was Monday, and the meetings could only happen on Thursdays, but Parth was relentless.

Raghav patiently pointed to Parth, "If you so insist, I will arrange a meeting with the Guide immediately, but then it would have to be your last meeting with him. There would never be another one. Those are the rules!"

Parth thought for a second and then said, without hesitation in his voice, "I understand that Raghav, but given the urgency of the situation, I would rather hear from the Guide one last time than lose a dear friend."

"Very well. Follow me, and I will take you to him for the last time. May you get the most out of your conversation," said Raghav, leading Parth to meet with the Guide.

Parth waited patiently outside the Guide's hut until both Raghav and the Guide walked out of it. Parth felt relieved the moment he saw the smile of the Guide. He then ended up conferring with the Guide for the longest time.

"We feel every bit of the energy we pass on to the world. If we spread anxiety and chaos, we must go through the same first. That is true for love, peace and happiness as well," Guide began after listening to the situation of Prishati in detail from Parth.

"Do as I say, and you will hopefully get back your friend," the Guide said, asking Parth to come closer. He then whispered something in his ear, which Raghav tried to hear but in vain.

"Thank you for everything, Guide!" Parth said with utmost gratitude, knowing that he would not be getting to see that wise figure ever again.

Parth rushed to grab his cell phone and called Yajur. "Book the next flight to Delhi. I am coming!"

"Sure, my friend! So glad to hear that!" Yajur exclaimed with enthusiasm.

"Send me the details. Got to call others too, catch you later!" Parth disconnected in a rush. Next, he called Kunal and Balveer.

"Meet me tomorrow morning outside Prishati's house. And yes, please bring some garbage from your house in a bag," Parth instructed.

Next morning, Kunal and Balveer picked up some trash, packed it in a black polybag and went straight to Prishati's house. There they met Parth, who was already waiting for them on the porch. They rang the bell, which obviously went unanswered. Prishati's car was in the driveway, and loud noise from a TV news debate could be heard outside.

"She is inside, but definitely not willing to let us in," Parth murmured to Kunal and Balveer. They told him they had been in this situation before. She did not answer their calls either.

Parth then pulled out the phone and started texting. "Hey Prishati, I am outside. If you don't talk to me now, I am going to spread all the garbage that I am carrying with me in your porch and your front yard. I will only count to 30; this is your last chance," Parth texted.

In about 30 seconds, and after almost a month since her last text, Prishati texted back, "Are you even here? That too with garbage? You are bluffing."

"You want to find out if I am bluffing or not, just come out and see for yourself," Parth responded, throwing an empty water bottle from his garbage bag onto the front yard.

Prishati peered through the window and saw Parth running around and littering her porch with vegetable peels, used bottles, wrappers, and all sorts of trash.

She immediately rushed out of the main door and stopped Parth from rummaging through his garbage bag.

Parth was relieved. He hugged Prishati, and then they both sat down.

"Are you mad, Parth? Who does all this? Now, you have to clean all this before you go," Prishati scolded in a soft tone.

"Look at you, Prishati! You could not tolerate a bag of trash on your porch even for a second but have welcomed so much rubbish news, data, media, etc. into your mind!" Parth said with a smile.

"Welcomed? She has given them permanent residency," Balveer laughed, coming closer.

"We can help you clean your house, but you will have to clean your mind yourself," Kunal pitched in too.

"Yes, Kunal will help you clean the house, but please clean up your mind," Balveer repeated, pushing Kunal a step forward.

"I am aware of what you are going through. I know the negativity of the world has got to you. The Guide told me that even if you put half a tablespoon of dirt in a glass of clean water, you need to put in an additional ten glasses of clean water in the same glass until that glass becomes clean again. Hence, now is not the time to self-confine yourself. Now is the time to surround yourself with the utmost positivity for the longest time. Now is the time to let the first light of the sun wake you up and help you make the best of every day and spread the goodness that you carry in your heart and your actions," Parth spoke with peace and compassion in his voice.

"It's easier said than done, guys. It is part of my profession," Prishati said in a helpless tone.

"Stop giving excuses, Prishati. Every inch of this planet experiences both the darkest of the night and the brightest of the day. It is up to you when and where you want to keep your eyes open," Kunal spoke with his recent experience.

"One more thing – Look at your garden. While you left it unattended for only a few days and see good plants have dried up, and weeds have spread all over. The mind is the same. You need to take in good content and pull out the toxicity on a daily basis. Even if left unattended for a few days, it will ruin your beautiful garden," Parth passed on the final words from the Guide.

"And don't stop us from helping you. Reach out anytime without any hesitation. We will be more than happy to help. Just like you see how Kunal will be helping you clean the house," Balveer said to lighten the mood.

Chapter 20

True Success

Parth's words of wisdom landed well with Prishati. She asked a lot of questions, which Parth could answer from his interactions with the Guide. One could see the guilt and worry vanish, and a beaming smile getting restored on Prishati's face.

She resumed her work and social life with newfound enthusiasm, actively seeking out the positivity that surrounded her and cherishing every act of kindness. Amazing stories and motivational events, which might have always existed but were now catching her attention, seemed to emerge everywhere. Committed to spreading real but optimistic news through her newspaper column, she ignited a ripple effect.

Gradually, her department was flooded with heartwarming stories: a son going the extra mile to help his father, a pet dog saving its owner's life, a community creating a green corridor for a heart patient, an NGO receiving an anonymous donation, a group of soldiers building a bridge to save villagers, a team of doctors performing life-saving surgery for a child free of cost and many more.

Prishati and her team diligently covered these stories, conducting interviews with everyday heroes, highlighting acts of bravery and honesty, family values, and animal welfare initiatives. This wave of positivity not only uplifted her team but inspired millions of readers, steering them towards a brighter and a more hopeful direction. It seemed people were longing for an authentic source of such positive news and inspiring insights from across the globe.

Her dedication did not go unnoticed; she received multiple awards and recognition for her work, eventually being promoted to a larger role.

Yajur and Balveer's vision for wellness blossomed into a flourishing chain of wellness centres, becoming a go-to haven for countless individuals seeking balance and rejuvenation in their lives. With each new centre they opened, the daily footfall soared, a testament to the profound impact they were making.

Their clientele was as diverse as their offerings, ranging from energetic teens to wise elders, all drawn to the inclusive and nurturing environment Yajur and Balveer cultivated. The centres thrived not just because of the services provided but because they created a community where everyone felt welcome and supported.

Kunal and Prishati excelled in promoting and marketing the wellness centres, effectively spreading the word and attracting the diverse clientele. Their innovative strategies and genuine passion for the cause not only boosted the centres' popularity but also brought them immense satisfaction in their respective careers. They were truly content, thriving in roles they were passionate about and making a positive impact on countless lives.

Sreejesh, leveraging his exceptional skills, developed a cutting-edge application that provided digital wellness solutions and seamlessly managed the operations of all the centres. His talent for innovation was evident as he assembled a dedicated team, many of whom were former students of Yajur. These were individuals whom Yajur had mentored and supported in securing admission to IITs, creating a beautiful cycle of mentorship and growth.

Parth's journey took a transformative turn as he emerged as a renowned speaker and author. His public lectures and talk shows touched millions of lives, inspiring change and promoting well-being. Taking over his father's pharmaceutical company, Parth ensured that authentic medications were available at reasonable costs, furthering his commitment to making a difference. His efforts not only revolutionised the company but also left a lasting impact on the health industry.

The friends, who once lacked purpose and were self-centred, focused only on profit, had now dedicated their lives to improving the lives of others. They were filled with empathy, compassion, and a sincere drive to make the world a better place. To their surprise, they discovered that their mission was being supported wholeheartedly by unknown individuals from all corners of the globe, contributing to their success in such a short span of time.

Chapter 21

The Guiding Voice

Back in the forest, after Parth left, Raghav questioned the Guide, "Why did you whisper in Parth's ear? Didn't you trust me with what you had to say?"

"I was explaining to him that filling our minds with trash and spreading it to others is a wrong practice. What I had to tell Parth about today's journalism and how to guide Prishati was relevant for him, but trash for you. Hence, I was practising what I preached," the Guide explained.

"Fair point. I have no business knowing what's happening in journalism and social media. But Parth has had his last visit and won't be able to see you again. Can't we do anything about that?" Raghav expressed his concern.

"My role was to set the wheel in motion. These friends have started their destined journey and my mission is over. They are more than capable of restoring a new era," the Guide affirmed.

"How can mere five individuals achieve such an enormous task? Are you sure you got your math right?" Raghav inquired with confusion evident on his face.

"Didn't I tell you about the great war of Kurukshetra? The epic of Mahabharata? Five righteous individuals stood victorious over a hundred rivals," the Guide paused, waiting for Raghav to recall. "Today, let me tell you what happened after the war was over," the Guide continued.

"After winning the war of Mahabharata, the five Pandavas ruled their kingdom for 36 years before deciding to renounce it and embark on their final journey. The Pandavas, along with Draupadi, embarked on this journey, known as the Mahaprasthana, or the 'great departure.' They left their kingdom and headed towards the Himalayas. On their way, they took shelter in a cave, as it was raining heavily that night. It was then that they began to worry about what would happen to all the knowledge they had acquired in their lifetime once they were gone. Arjun recalled that life is energy, and energy can neither be created nor destroyed – it only changes form. So, the five brothers decided to scribble all they knew on the walls of the cave, hoping to find it in their future lives, when it would matter the most," the Guide paused again.

"You mean... they are... what are you saying?" Raghav sat down with his eyes wide open. "That explains why they could understand so much and so easily from those scribbles and wall carvings. It was written by them and for themselves. It all makes sense now," he added. "How about Prishati?"

"Do you know, Draupadi's grandfather's name was Prishat? Can you see the connection?" the Guide questioned.

"Hmm... interesting! Though I understand they are powerful souls, I still feel we should continue to help them," Raghav suggested.

"I understand. Even back then, you empowered them not by fighting in the war, but by sharing the knowledge of the Universe. That's exactly what you need to do now. You guided them, provided the necessary knowledge, and now it's time for them to fight their own battles. Besides, just as the Pandavas had millions supporting them, these five will find their own allies in this life," the Guide reassured.

"How will they recognise their millions of allies?" Raghav asked.

"It's tricky to identify who the incarnations of their former allies are today. Over time, forms have changed drastically, but the energy remains the same. Did you not sense these friends' vibes when you first met them? These millions of energies, ready to support their mission of bringing a new and beautiful era, could be anywhere and anyone – even the one reading this book."

Raghav looked puzzled. "Which book?"

The Guide turned and gave you—the reader—that smile. Returning his attention to Raghav, a hint of mischief in his eyes, he said, "Ah, Raghav, always the curious one. You are the reincarnated Vāsudeva, the one who guides and cares for his people."

Raghav's eyes widened in surprise. "Me? Then who are you?"

"I am the knowledge of the Universe, the Guiding Voice, the positive energy omnipresent inside each individual," echoed the voice. With that, the Guide's form began to shimmer and glow. He split into millions of tiny, bright sparks, each a fragment of his essence. The sparks danced in the air, filling the chamber with a radiant light, before spreading and entering the bodies of millions across the globe, including the five friends and Raghav himself.

Raghav watched in awe as the Guide's energy merged with him, feeling a surge of warmth and enlightenment.

The Guide's voice echoed one last time, "Remember, the true power lies not in the knowledge you possess, but in how you choose to use it."

www.ingramcontent.com/pod-product-compliance
Lightning Source LLC
LaVergne TN
LVHW091113150826
845673LV00002B/805

* 9 7 9 8 8 9 6 1 0 3 7 0 7 *